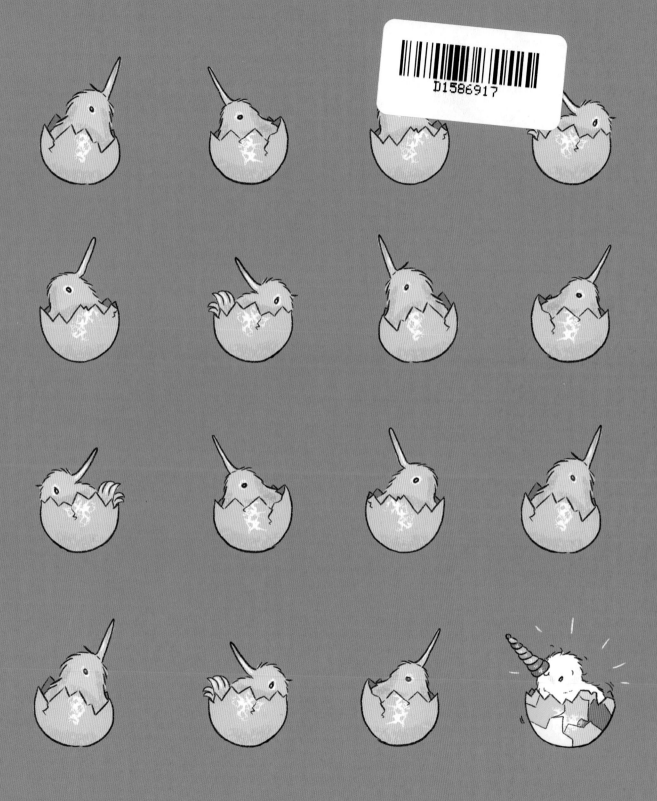

The EXTRAORDINARY human
who owns this book is:

Who is STRONG,
SASSY and SMART?

KIWICORN!

I read, write, paint and play.
I am building a powerful mind.

Who is GENTLE, GUTSY and GOOD-HEARTED?

KIWICORN!

I care about others
and they care about me.

Who is CONFIDENT, CUTE and COLOURFULLY CREATIVE?

KIWICORN!

I am so flamboyant,
I could float away.

Who is WILD, WISPY and often WHIFFY?

Who is WHIMSICAL, WITTY and WONDERFULLY WEIRD?

KIWICORN!

I love being different,
because different is never dull.

Who is RADICAL, RADIANT and REBELLIOUS ?

KIWICORN!

EQUAL RIGHTS FOR ALL!

I speak out and stand up
for what I believe.

Who is DASHING, DELIGHTFUL, and sometimes a little DOWN?

KIWICORN!

I know that if I have a bad day,
happiness isn't too far away.

Who is POLITE, PEACEFUL and a PLANET PROTECTOR?

KIWICORN!

I am a tree hugger, and
I like a good flower hug too.

I am an INCREDIBLE,
INDEPENDENT individual.

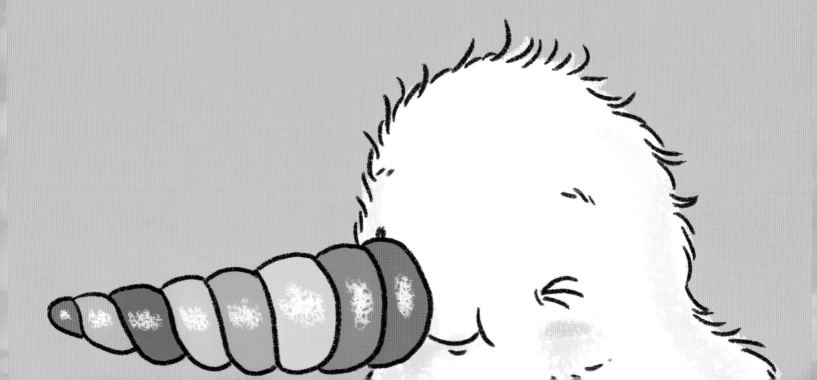

JUST LIKE YOU!

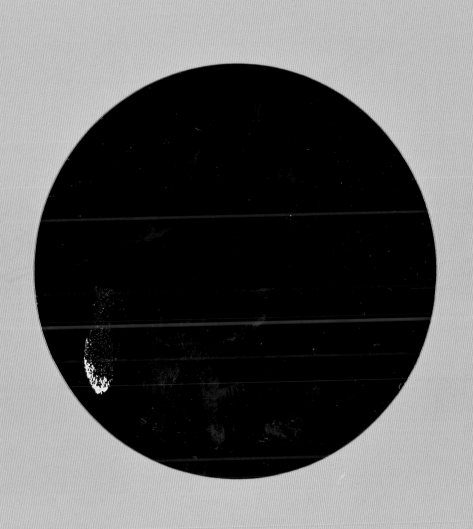

For Opal, Willow and Florence.
Always let your uniqueness shine!

- - - - Kat

Kat Merewether is an award-winning author and illustrator residing in Te Awamutu, a quaint town nestled in the central North Island of New Zealand.

Kat gains inspiration and critique from her own brood of three sparkling daughters. Her sweet yet empowering characters and storylines charm readers of all ages around the globe.

Kat is a passionate ambassador for Kiwis for Kiwi, the charity protecting the flightless bird, native to New Zealand.

The iconic and precious kiwi is endangered, with an estimated 75,000 remaining. The kiwi is the star of Kiwicorn, an endearing story about being unique.